PAPA'S LEMONADE

Greenwillow
Read-alone

GREENWILLOW BOOKS

EVE RICE

PAPA'S LEMONADE

AND OTHER STORIES

A DIVISION OF WILLIAM MORROW & COMPANY, INC. | NEW YORK

For HHR,
with all my love

1   2   3   4   5   80   79   78   77   76

Library of Congress Cataloging in Publication Data
Rice, Eve.   Papa's lemonade and other stories.
(Greenwillow read-alone)   Contents: Pennies.—A garden.
—A nice walk.—Missing.—Papa's lemonade. [1. Family life—Fiction.
2. Short stories]   I. Title.   PZ7.R3622Pap   [E]   75-38754
ISBN 0-688-80041-6   ISBN 0-688-84041-8 lib. bdg.

CONTENTS

PENNIES

Papa walked into the kitchen.

He had been shopping.

"Papa, Papa! Do you have

any pennies?" asked Freddie.

"Pennies?" said Molly.

"Pennies?" said Sam.

"Does Papa have pennies?"
asked Nora.

And a little voice said,

"Oh, goodie! Pennies!" It was Jasper.

"Now, now," said Mama. "At least

let Papa put his things down."

Papa put the bags on the table.

He looked in his pockets for pennies.

"Here," he said.

Papa had a handful of pennies.

He gave each of the children two.

Freddie put his pennies
in his bank—"clink, clink."
Molly dropped hers in.
"Clink, clink."
And Sam. And Nora.

Jasper dropped his pennies in his bank.
And then something awful happened.

Jasper dropped his bank.

And there he stood,

in the middle of all his pennies.

Jasper sniffled.

"Don't cry," said Papa.

"Don't cry," said Mama.

"We will find you a new bank.

Let me see."

Mama took a big bottle

down from the shelf.

"Does this look like a bank

for Jasper?"

"No," said Sam.

"Uh, uh," said Molly.

And Jasper sniffled again.

So Mama put it back.

She took down
a square tin.
"Is this a bank?"
"No," said Freddie.
"It's a cooky tin."

"How about this?"
asked Mama.
"It's a sugar bowl,"
said Nora.
Jasper frowned.

Mama thought hard.
"There must be
a bank for Jasper
somewhere."

She moved the ketchup and the sugar.

"Here it is!" she said.

Mama had an empty honey jar
shaped like a little bear.

"A bear bank for Jasper?"

Jasper smiled. "A bear bank!"

"A bear bank is a fine bank," said Papa,
"and every bit as good as a piggy bank."

Mama gave the bear bank to Jasper.

Then Mama and Papa,

Molly, Freddie, Nora, Sam, and Jasper

picked up all the pennies.

They put them in Jasper's new bank.

"There," said Mama.

"There," said Jasper.

"There," said Papa. "And what
a nice family of banks we have—
four little pigs and one fine bear."

A GARDEN

When they had picked up the bits
of Jasper's old bank, Mama said,
"It's too nice a day to stay inside.
Why don't you go out and play?"
"It's too hot," said Freddie.
"I don't want to," Molly said.

"Me neither," said Sam.

"Uh, uh," said Nora.

Jasper didn't say a word.

"All right," Papa said.

"Mama and I are going outside."

"Good-bye!" called Mama and Papa
as they walked out the door.

"Good-bye," called the children.

Mama and Papa
stood in the sunshine.
"Wouldn't it be nice to have
a garden?" Mama asked.
"Yes, indeed," said Papa.
"We could plant a garden
by the cherry tree.
I will get a shovel."

"Wait," said Mama. "We have nothing
   to put in our garden yet."

"True," Papa said.

"But we can dig out the rocks.
   Good gardens don't have rocks."

"First, let's think
   what we will plant.
   Then we can dig," said Mama.

They sat down under the cherry tree
and closed their eyes to think better.

"Strawberries," said Mama after a minute.

"Mmmmmm. Strawberries," said Papa.

"That will be nice.

We can have strawberries

like the ones that grow in the woods."

"Yes," Mama said. "And what else?"

"Grapes," said Papa.

"For jam," Mama said. "Jam grapes

like the ones that grow by the lake."

"And what else?" asked Papa.

"Onions—the kind that grow
along the road.
Then we can make onion soup."

"I love onion soup," Papa said,

"and carrots too."

"Mmmmmm. Like the wild carrots
from the field," said Mama.

She thought some more.

"You know?" she said.

"What?" asked Papa.

"We don't really need a garden at all.
What we need is a nice walk
along the road, across the field,
and down to the lake."

"Good idea," said Papa.

"And then I don't need a shovel.

But I do need my walking stick."

"And I will take my basket,"

Mama said, "to fill with good things

along the way."

A NICE WALK

It took Papa a little while
to find his walking stick.
Then they were ready.

Mama and Papa
walked down the road.
Mama swung her basket.

They walked past a little house.

"Hello! Nice day!" called a skunk.

"Hello to you," said Mama and Papa.

"We are off on a walk
down to the lake."

"Have a nice walk," said the skunk.

"Have a nice day," said Mama and Papa.

And off they went across the field.

A rabbit came hopping.

"Well, hello there," said Mama.

"Hello, hello," the rabbit said.

"Lovely grass for nibbling here."

"We're going down to the lake,"
said Papa.

"Have a nice time," said the rabbit.

"And good day to you," Mama said.

They walked on into the woods.

They passed an old tree.

Two squirrels poked their heads out.

"Hello!"

"Hello!"

"What a fine tree," said Mama.

"Stop and have some tea?"

"We're on our way down to the lake,"
Papa said.

"Well, have a nice walk then,"
the squirrel said.

"Thank you!" called Mama and Papa
over their shoulders. "Good-bye!"

Mama and Papa came to the lake.

They dipped their paws in the water

and made ripples.

Then they walked home.

"Oh, I'm tired," said Mama.

"I am too," said Papa

and sat on the front step.

Mama put her basket down.

"Oh, Papa! I was so busy

saying hello that I forgot

all about the carrots!"

"And I forgot too," said Papa.

"No strawberries either," said Mama.

"No grapes. No onions.

Now we cannot make onion soup."

"No onion soup," said Papa.
"But we had a nice walk
and we have nice friends.
And that's even better than
onion soup."

MISSING

When Papa had rested a minute,

he felt better.

Mama got up and opened the door.

"Something is strange," she said.

"What?" asked Papa.

"I am quite sure it is too quiet

for a house with five children."

Papa listened.

It was very quiet.

"Yes," said Papa.

"I think there are no children

in this house at all."

"No children—but lots of paw prints,"

said Mama.

"Aha!" Papa said.

"Let's see where they go."

Mama and Papa

followed the tracks.

The paw prints stopped

at the back door.

Papa opened the door.

"There they are. They are sitting

on the rock," said Mama.

"But I do not think they are all there."

She counted heads.

"One, two, three, four . . . four.

We are missing a child."

"Missing?" said Papa. "Let me count.

One, two, three, four.

Yes," Papa said.

"We are missing a child."

"Now," said Mama. "Who is missing?"

"Who is missing?" said Papa.

"Who is missing?" said a little voice.

Mama and Papa turned around.

There was Jasper.

"That is the child

who is missing," said Mama.

"The missing child," Papa said.

"I am not missing," said Jasper.

"I am right here."

"You are indeed," said Papa.

"So now we can stop looking.

And since I don't have to look
for you, I can make some lemonade."

"Lemonade?" said Jasper. "Mmmm."

"Fine," Mama said.

"We can all have lemonade."

"Children!" called Mama.

Not an ear twitched.

"Lemonade!" Mama called.

And all the ears turned.

"Wow! Lemonade!"

And they all came running.

PAPA'S LEMONADE

Everyone went into the kitchen.

"Now for the lemonade," said Papa.

He went to get the lemons.

"No lemons?" asked Papa.

"There are oranges,

but I do not see any lemons.

Where have they all gone?"

"Jasper ate them" said Molly.

"That's silly," said Mama.

Mama looked at Jasper.

Jasper looked a little sour.

"Jasper, did you eat the lemons?"

Jasper would not look at Mama

or Papa so they all knew

that he had eaten the lemons.

"Oh, Jasper!" said Mama.

"That is very hard to believe."

"Yes," said Papa.

"And it is very hard to make
lemonade without any lemons.
But I will try."

Papa got the oranges.

He squeezed them into a jug.

Then he added water

and sugar and stirred it all.

"Now," he said, "lemonade!"

"Orangeade," whispered Nora.

"I heard that," Papa said.

He filled the glasses

and sat down.

"Now," Papa said, "we will all
   think very lemon thoughts."
"Sour," said Sam.
   They all took a sip.
"It tastes like orange juice,"
   said Freddie.

"You are not thinking hard enough,"
Papa said.

"Think more lemon thoughts."

"Yellow," Molly said.

"Very, very sour," said Nora.

"Shiny, bumpy outside," said Freddie.

"Doesn't roll right," said Jasper.

Molly looked at Jasper.

"Well, it doesn't," Jasper said.

"It isn't round."

"Lemony lemonade," said Mama.

"Lemony lemonade," they all said
and took another sip.

"Maybe it does taste a little
like lemonade," Nora said.
"A little? It tastes a lot
like lemonade!" said Papa.

Mama laughed.

"It is the best lemonade made with oranges that I have ever had."

They all laughed.

And they all took another sip . . .

and another . . .

and another . . .

and finished Papa's lemonade

right down to the very last drop.